Merry Christmas, Dear Dragon

MODERN CURRICULUM PRESS

Pearson Learning Group

Merry Christmas, Dear Dragon

Margaret Hillert

Illustrated by Carl Kock

ISBN: 0-8136-5526-9 (paperback)
ISBN: 0-8136-5026-7 (hardbound)

Printed in the United States of America
    16 17 18 19 20   08 07

3 1984 00265 1808

Modern
Curriculum
Press
Pearson Learning Group

1-800-821-3106
www.pearsonlearning.com

Look at this.

Down, down it comes.

What fun.

What fun.

But it is work, too.
I will have to work.
I can make it go away.

6

Oh, my.
Look at you.
You can help me.
What a big help you are.

8

We can play, too.
It is fun to play in this.
Run, run, run.
And jump, jump, jump.

We can make something big.
Big, big, big.
See, see.
It looks like you!

Oh, oh.
Look at that car.
It can not go.

You can help.
Work, work, work.
Now it can go away.
That is good.

12

13

Now come with me.
We have to get something.
Something for the house.

Look here. Look here.
Here is the one we want.
Not too little.
Not too big.

15

Mother. Mother
See me ride.
Look what we have.
16 It is for the house.

I see it.
I like it.
It is a good one.
Come in. Come in.

18

See what we can make.
Cookies. Cookies.
Look at this —
        and this —
                and this.

One for me.
And one for you.
A big, big one for you!

Now we will do this.
Here are some balls.
This is fun.
I like to do this.

You can help with this one.
Make it go up.
Up, up, up.

Where are you now?
Where did you go?
I can not guess.
24   I can not find you.

Come here.
Come here.
I want you.
I like you here with me.

25

Oh, here you are!
I see you now.
Look at you.
You are funny.

26

27

Here is something.

I can not make it work.

You will have to do it for me.

Oh, my. Oh, my.
Look at it now.
Red and yellow.
I like this. 29

Here you are with me.

And here I am with you.

Oh, what a merry Christmas, dear dragon.

Margaret Hillert, author of several books in the MCP Beginning-To-Read Series, is a writer, poet, and teacher.

Merry Christmas, Dear Dragon uses the 69 words listed below.

a	father	like	see
am	find	little	something
and	for	look(s)	
are	fun		that
at	funny	make	the
away		me	this
	get	merry	to
balls	go	mother	too
big	good	my	
but	guess		want
		not	we
can	have	now	what
car	help		where
Christmas	here	oh	will
come(s)	house	one	with
cookies			work
	I	play	
dear	in		yellow
did	is	red	you
do	it	ride	
down		run	
dragon	jump